Right Where You Are

By Jared Goodykoontz

~ Second Edition ~

LABC Book #2

This book is
dedicated to:

My God
My Wife
My Daughter
My Land

Jared Goodykoontz loves God's handiwork:
natural spaces and smiling faces.
Bringing those two together brings Jared much joy!
He has been blessed to run the
Little Adventures Big Connections nature program
in Columbus, OH since 2017.

This book was made on (and with bits of) the
beautiful 6 acre property Jared calls home.

This is Grumpus the Mushroom. These days he enjoys two things:
being grumpy, and enjoying some alone time at his Magic Spot.

This is Mooshy Moo. She's Grumpus' sister and pretty much loves everything.

Grumpus had seen Deer tracks on his way to his Magic Spot. He took his sister to them, hoping she'd stay there while he enjoyed some more peace and quiet back on his favorite log.

So... where's the next track?

After thinking for a moment, Mooshy Moo had an idea:

Sometimes you have to BECOME the animal to figure out the story of where they've gone.

Grumpus thought she was being pretty weird... but he couldn't help but wonder if the next track was over there.

After Mooshy Moo's lesson, Grumpus determined their Deer friend was headed South down a ravine. The two found all sorts of clues:

Muddy Deer Track

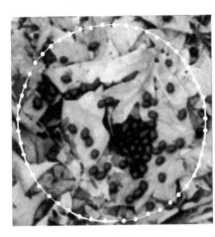
Deer Scat

Deer Browse Marks

...crossed the stream!

SPLASH

What are those dots at the back?

5 minutes later...

Grass! Perfect for both!

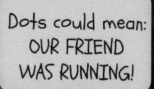

Dots could mean: OUR FRIEND WAS RUNNING!

pant

Phew! I'm tired. I need a snack and a nap!

The next morning...

It was Grumpus' turn to be the Deer now. He decided to climb a nearby stump to better see the next track...

crunch

crupch

Mooshy Moo followed. Suddenly she heard her brother from the top:

WHOA.

I'm coming!

Extension Ideas
Try these out on your own and with your family and friends!

On To The Next One

Sometimes you find a trail of animal tracks the ends suddenly. Where's the next track? Try measuring the distance between two tracks earlier in the trail.
Now measure that same distance starting at the last track you could find.
You can try all directions. Did you find any tracks or sign?
Remember Mooshy Moo's tip: "The toes tell where they go!"

Watch & Be

If you see an animal outside or at the zoo, watch how they stand. How do they move their heads? Their bodies? Their feet? Do they do any movement repetitively? Are they slow or fast? Are they smooth or jerky movers? Try to copy their movements. Think: "What would be important to this animal?" Try this with local wild animals you want to track.
(Online Videos can work too!)

Best Places To Find Tracks

* Where two habitats meet
* Near a water source
* Near a food source or shelter

For More Mooshy Moo & Grumpus Books

Go to facebook.com/jgoodstories for updates, activities, and to order Mooshy Moo & Grumpus books about Observation, Bird Language and more!

Great Books About Tracking

*Traces by Paula Fox
*In the Snow by Sharon Phillips Denslow
*WILD TRACKS! by Jim Arnosky
*Crinkleroot Guide to Animal Tracking by Jim Arnosky
For more advanced:
*Any and all books by Tom Brown, Jr.

CPSIA information can be obtained
at www.ICGtesting.com
Printed in the USA
LVHW071050170421
684658LV00004B/12